SUPER GRAMMAR

Learn Grammar with Superheroes

Written by	Illustrated by
Tony Preciado	**Rhode Montijo**

Super Examples colored by Jenny Hansen
Additional Super Examples inked by Joe To

Copyright © 2012 by Tony Preciado and Rhode Montijo

All rights reserved. Published by Scholastic Inc. SCHOLASTIC and associated logos are trademarks and/or registered trademarks of Scholastic Inc.

ISBN 978-0-545-42515-5

10 9 8 7 6 5 4 3 2 1   12 13 14 15 16 17/0

Printed in the U.S.A.   40
First printing, September 2012

Scholastic Inc.

Table of Contents

A Call to All Citizens!

Dear citizen, we need your help in the fight for grammar.

A good hero fights only for something that he or she believes in. So, before you can decide to fight for grammar, you should understand exactly what grammar is.

Grammar is the all-powerful set of super rules that help us make strong and correct sentences. With grammar we can use words, phrases, clauses, and punctuation to create powerful sentences whenever we need them.

And now, citizen, if you believe that your words are important, and if you believe in having strong sentences, and if you believe in protecting your words from errors and mistakes—then *Super Grammar* has a mission for you.

The Mission!

Since the beginning of time, grammar has been on a mission. This mission has been to keep all sentences correct and free of wrongdoing.

This mission has not always been easy, but grammar believes that every sentence, no matter its message, no matter its size, and no matter its complexity, is worth fighting for. So that's exactly what grammar does; grammar fights to keep all of our sentences correct.

Now, you might be wondering, "What is grammar fighting against?"

Well, citizen, grammar is fighting against the sworn enemies of correct grammar: The Sabotage Squad, also known as grammar mistakes. This rotten bunch of sentence supervillains is always fighting against correct grammar, and they don't like to play by the rules. They will lie, cheat, and steal if they have to. They will confound, confuse, and mislead you at every turn. Whatever it takes to ruin your sentences, this nasty bunch of grammar mistakes will do it.

Because of the Sabotage Squad, grammar is constantly under attack, and unfortunately, grammar can't fight off all of these supervillains all by itself. The only way for grammar to stand a chance in defeating these unruly wrongdoers is with your help.

That's right; grammar wants *you* to join the fight. And the best way for you to join this fight and help grammar protect your sentences is by accepting this special assignment: *The Super Grammar Mission.*

However, before you decide to accept this mission, you should know that fighting for correct grammar isn't going to be easy. Mistakes are hiding around every corner, and they're always waiting for their chance to attack; so take heed, citizen—this is not a battle for the weak.

It takes bravery and courage to confront the relentless mob of villains that cause grammar mistakes, and it takes a strong commitment to prevail in showing them the error of their ways.

But have no fear, citizen. For even though fighting for correct grammar is tough, if you decide to accept this mission, you will not be alone. . . .

Behold the Heroes of Super Grammar!

These brave superheroes are the guardians of correct grammar, and together they use their amazing superpowers to protect and defend your sentences from the troublesome grammar villains who love to cause grammar mistakes.

And even now, as you stand in the face of foul fragments, rotten run-ons, and cowardly comma splices—the superheroes of *Super Grammar* will always stand by your side as you fight your never-ending battle between good and bad grammar!

Now, citizen, before you decide to accept this mission you should understand exactly what is expected of you.

The Super Grammar Mission, should you choose to accept it, is to learn everything about the Super Grammar superheroes. Learn their names, powers, their teams, and how they work together.

On this mission, learning about the Super Grammar superheroes will be the top priority.

These superheroes have the power to defend and protect your sentences from mistakes. It's important to know all about each superhero's strengths and weaknesses, so that when the time comes, you'll know *when*, *how*, and *why* you're calling them into action.

The more you know, the stronger your defense will be—and the better you'll be able to protect your sentences against malicious mistakes.

Each superhero belongs to a Super Grammar super-team, and there are three superhero super-teams:

1. **THE COMPLETION TEAM!** (Parts of a Sentence):
These superheroes help you make complete sentences that are fearless and strong.

2. **THE AMAZING EIGHT!** (Parts of Speech):
These superheroes are an elite group of power-enhanced words that use their amazing abilities to improve your sentences.

3. **THE SUPER SYMBOLS!** (Punctuation Marks):
These superheroes use their unique and special codes to keep your sentences super clear, super organized, and super correct.

Also, in order to complete this mission, you'll have to learn about one last super-team. But the members of this group are not superheroes at all; they're the supervillains.

4. **THE SABOTAGE SQUAD!** (Grammar Mistakes):
The sinister members of this group are bent on breaking your sentences at any cost. Whatever it takes to foul up your sentences, they'll do it.

If you decide to accept this mission, you'll learn that all three of the Super Grammar super-teams are dedicated to the task of protecting your sentences, and you'll also learn that every supervillain is out to ruin them by stealing your sentence correctness.

Also, you'll learn that the only way to successfully complete this mission is by using teamwork—and not just on the part of the superheroes, but also from you. Because even though every superhero is ready to fight for your sentence correctness, it's only going to work if you are part of the team, too.

So, citizen, now that you know everything about this special assignment, will you do it? Will you accept the Super Grammar Mission?

If so . . .

WELCOME TO THE TEAM!

After you complete the Super Grammar Mission, you, the superheroes, and all of your sentences will be ready to win the fight!

THE COMPLETION TEAM!

THE COMPLETION TEAM MEMBERS:

- THE SUBJECT
- THE PREDICATE

THE SUBJECT AND PREDICATE CAN JOIN FORCES:
- THE POWER OF COMPLETE SENTENCES

With only two members, the Completion Team is the smallest of the three super-teams, but that doesn't mean that they don't have a big and important role to play in keeping your sentences strong and correct. In fact, these two superheroes may very well have the most important grammar job of all: making complete sentences.

Now, citizen, you might be wondering, "Why are complete sentences so important?"

Well, think about it this way: If you were a super crime-fighter, would you go into battle with only **half** of your body armor?

No, you wouldn't—because you'd get clobbered if you did that!

Well, it's the exact same thing with sentences: They need *both* sides of their armor, the Subject and the Predicate, in order to be complete. And if sentences don't have their complete armor, they'll get *completely* clobbered by the Sabotage Squad.

But once a sentence is fully complete, that sentence is ready to test its super protective armor against any grammar mistake that dares to attack it, because a *complete sentence* is a strong sentence.

SO, CITIZEN, IT'S TIME FOR YOU TO JOIN FORCES WITH THE COMPLETION TEAM AND LEARN ALL ABOUT THEIR SUPERPOWERS. AND AFTER THAT, YOUR SUPER PROTECTIVE SENTENCE ARMOR WILL BE COMPLETE!

THE SUBJECT!

This superhero is the main focus of every true sentence, and as a member of the Completion Team, the Subject uses all of his powers to make sure that every sentence is always talking about him.

Being the center of attention isn't as easy as it sounds. It takes power to bear the weight of being the subject of a sentence. So, to help him with his task, the Subject has several powers.

His main power is the one that helps him act as the subject of a sentence. But the Subject is also equipped with three other powers that enable him to be the most effective and versatile subject possible. These powers are called: the power of Number, the power of Compound, and the power of Invisibility.

WITH THESE POWERS, THE SUBJECT WILL ALWAYS BE READY TO DO HIS PART IN KEEPING YOUR SENTENCES STRONG AND COMPLETE.

POWERS OF THE SUBJECT:

1. THE SUBJECT'S MAIN POWER
2. THE POWER OF NUMBER
3. THE POWER OF COMPOUND
4. THE POWER OF INVISIBILITY

THE SUBJECT'S MAIN POWER!

Every complete sentence needs a subject—a main character—and the Subject's main superpower allows him to be the person, place, or thing that the sentence is telling us something about.

Here's an example:

The hero fights crime.

The subject of this sentence is "The hero" because "The hero" is the person, place, or thing that the sentence is telling us something about.

Without a subject, this sentence wouldn't have *anybody* or *anything* to talk about, and that would make it incomplete and incorrect, so it's important to check and make sure that your sentences always include a subject.

To find the subject of a sentence, ask yourself: Which person, place, or thing is the sentence telling us something about?

Using the same example sentence, "The hero fights crime," we can find the subject by asking this question: Which person, place, or thing fights crime?

The hero fights crime.

The answer is "The hero" because "The hero" is the person, place, or thing that "fights crime."

SUPERPOWER:

THE SUBJECT HAS THE POWER TO BE A PERSON, PLACE, OR THING THAT THE PREDICATE OF A SENTENCE IS TELLING US SOMETHING ABOUT.

SUPER EXAMPLES:

Mr. Powerhouse can lift a lot of weight.

Which person, place, or thing can lift a lot of weight? The subject is a *person*:

Mr. Powerhouse

The city is protected.

Which person, place, or thing is protected? The subject is a *place*:

The city

SUPER EXAMPLES:

The time bomb is ticking.

Which person, place, or thing is ticking? The subject is a *thing* (tangible/concrete):

The time bomb

Greed is a powerful force.

Which person, place, or thing is a powerful force? The subject is a *thing* (abstract):

Greed

THE SUBJECT'S POWER OF NUMBER!

When you think of the Subject, you probably think of him as only a singular superhero, but the Subject has the power of Number, and this power allows him to be either singular or plural.

Here's an example:

The diamond is missing.

The subject of this sentence, "The diamond," is singular.

But if we use the Subject's power of Number, we can make this subject plural by simply adding an *s* to the end, like this:

The diamonds are missing.

Now our subject, "The diamonds," is plural.

Most singular subjects can be made plural by simply adding a letter *s* to the end, like this:

muscle → muscles

But subjects already ending with an *s*, as well as subjects that end in *ch* or *x*, need to be made plural by adding *es* to the end, like this:

weakness → weaknesses
punch → punches
cash box → cash boxes

Also, take caution, citizen, for there are a handful of words that are irregular, and they don't follow the standard way of changing singular subjects into plurals, such as these:

knife ➔ knives
fungus ➔ fungi
mouse ➔ mice

If you ever have any doubt about changing a singular subject into its plural form, the right thing to do is look it up!

So, citizen, now you know about the Subject's power of Number. It allows us to change the *number* of our subjects from singular to plural, and that gives our sentences the super flexibility they need to communicate more effectively about people, places, and things that are more than one.

SUPERPOWER:

THE POWER OF NUMBER GIVES THE SUBJECT THE POWER TO BE SINGULAR OR PLURAL.

SUPER EXAMPLES:

The meteor is hurling toward Earth!

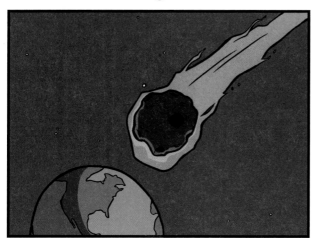

Meteor: singular

meteor

The meteors are hurling toward Earth!

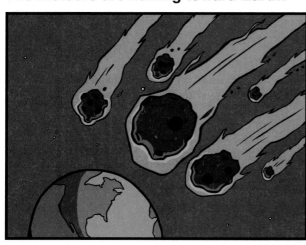

Meteors: plural
(made plural by
adding an *s*)

meteors

The witness described the crime scene.

witness: singular

witness

The witnesses described the crime scene.

witnesses: plural (made plural by adding *es*)

witnesses

THE SUBJECT'S POWER OF COMPOUND!

The Subject has the power of Compound. Compound means two or more different parts, and this power allows a sentence to have two or more different subjects in the same sentence.

Without compound subjects, we would have to write a separate sentence for each individual subject, like this:

Muscle Spasm is a powerful superhero.
Strong Arm is a powerful superhero.
Brute Force is a powerful superhero.

Writing sentences in this way would be repetitive and wasteful.

But by using the Subject's power of Compound, a single sentence can have multiple subjects that all share the same predicate, like this:

Muscle Spasm, Strong Arm, and Brute Force are powerful superheroes.

Each subject, "Muscle Spasm," "Strong Arm," and "Brute Force," is listed together as a group, and this lets them all share the same predicate of the sentence ("are powerful superheroes"), but because the subjects are all separated by a comma (,) we can recognize each one as a separate and different item in the list.

The Subject's power of Compound is a very useful power. It allows two or more different subjects in the same sentence, and this helps to keep our sentences superefficient and super organized.

SUPERPOWER:

THE SUBJECT HAS THE POWER OF COMPOUND, AND THIS POWER ALLOWS A SENTENCE TO HAVE TWO OR MORE DIFFERENT SUBJECTS.

SUPER EXAMPLES:

Turtle-man and Super-snail each carry their own secret hideout.

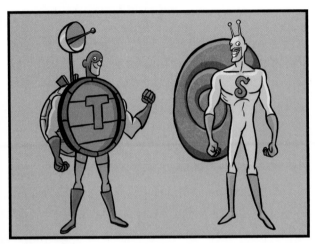

compound subjects (two):

Turtle-man and Super-snail

Truth, honor, and justice will always prevail.

compound subjects (three):

Truth, honor, and justice

THE SUBJECT'S POWER OF INVISIBILITY!

You can't have a complete sentence without the Subject, but just because you can't see the Subject, it doesn't always mean that he's not really there—especially if the Subject is using his amazing power of Invisibility!

The Subject has the power of Invisibility, but he can only use this power on sentences that are *commands* or *requests*.

Here are some examples:

Help me.   Look out!   Stop!

Each of these sentences, which are commands or requests, has a subject. You just can't see them because these subjects are invisible.

If we reveal these invisible subjects, you'll be able to see who the subject of each sentence is. Take a look:

You, help me.   You, look out!   You, stop!

The subject of each of these sentences is "you."

Here's why the subject is "you": Whenever anyone makes a command or request, they are directing the command or request toward a second person or persons.

SUPERPOWER:

THE SUBJECT HAS THE POWER TO BECOME INVISIBLE IN SENTENCES THAT ARE COMMANDS OR REQUESTS.

In English, the second person pronoun (see pg. 50) is always "you," so this means that whenever anyone makes a command or request, we can always be sure that the pronoun "you" will be the subject of that sentence. And since the second person pronoun, "you," can be either singular or plural, it can work for commands or requests that are addressing either one single person or several hundred people.

That's why the second person pronoun, "you," makes a perfect invisible subject!

And now that we all understand that "you" is always the perfect subject for any command or request, we don't have to actually see a visible subject anymore. The subject can now be invisible, and we can all just know that the invisible subject is always "you."

The Subject's power of Invisibility is a very practical power. It allows important and urgent commands and requests to be short and direct, which can be a big time-saver, and also a lifesaver, especially if you're ever in trouble and need to call for "Help!"

FINDING THE INVISIBLE SUBJECT:

YOU DON'T NEED X-RAY VISION TO FIND THE INVISIBLE SUBJECT. YOU JUST NEED TO REMEMBER THESE TWO THINGS:
1. THE SUBJECT CAN ONLY BE INVISIBLE IN COMMANDS OR REQUESTS.
2. IT'S UNDERSTOOD THAT THE INVISIBLE SUBJECT IS ALWAYS *YOU*.

SUPER EXAMPLES:

Hold it right there!

(invisible) subject:

you

Freeze!

(invisible) subject:

you

THE PREDICATE!

The Predicate is the official voice of every sentence, and as a member of the Completion Team, the Predicate uses her voice and superpowers to clearly communicate something about the Subject.

Being the official voice of every sentence is a big and awesome responsibility, but the Predicate is a skilled and fearless communicator. And, aside from having exceptional communication skills, the Predicate is also equipped with a couple of superpowers that help her in getting her message across.

Her main power is the one that helps her act as the predicate of a sentence. And her second ability, the power of Compound, helps her to be the most effective predicate possible.

WITH THESE TWO POWERS, THE PREDICATE WILL ALWAYS BE READY TO DO HER PART IN KEEPING YOUR SENTENCES STRONG AND COMPLETE.

POWERS OF THE PREDICATE:

1. THE PREDICATE'S MAIN POWER
2. THE POWER OF COMPOUND

THE PREDICATE'S MAIN POWER!

The Predicate's main power gives her the ability to communicate something to us about the subject.

Here's an example:

The thief robbed the bank.

The predicate of this sentence is "robbed the bank" because it is the part of the sentence that is communicating something about the subject.

It's important to check that your sentences always include a predicate.

To find the predicate of a sentence, ask yourself: "What is the sentence communicating about the subject?"

Using the same example sentence, "The thief robbed the bank," we can find the predicate by asking the question like this: What is the sentence communicating to us about the thief?

The thief robbed the bank.

The answer is "robbed the bank," because that's what the sentence is communicating about the subject.

SUPERPOWER:

THE POWER OF THE PREDICATE ALLOWS THE PREDICATE TO COMMUNICATE SOMETHING TO US ABOUT THE SUBJECT OF A SENTENCE.

SUPER EXAMPLES:

The evil scientist invented a new weapon.

What is this sentence communicating about the subject?

predicate:

invented a new weapon

The cat burglar is stealing cats.

What is this sentence communicating about the subject?

predicate:

is stealing cats

THE PREDICATE'S POWER OF COMPOUND!

Similar to the Subject's ability, the Predicate also has the power of Compound. Compound means two or more different parts, and this power allows a sentence to have two or more different predicates for the same subject.

Without compound predicates, we would have to write a separate sentence for each individual predicate.

Here are some examples:

The superhero smashed the weapon.
The superhero saved the hostage.
The superhero caught the bad guy.

But by using the Predicate's power of Compound, a single sentence can have two or more different predicates that all share the same subject. Like this:

The superhero smashed the weapon, saved the hostage, and caught the bad guy.

All three predicates, "smashed the weapon," "saved the hostage," and "caught the bad guy," are listed together as a group, and this lets them all share the same subject of the sentence ("The superhero"), but because the predicates are all separated by a comma (,) we can recognize each one as a separate and different item in the list.

The Predicate's power of Compound is a very useful power, because it helps to keep our sentences superefficient and super organized.

SUPERPOWER:

THE PREDICATE HAS THE POWER OF COMPOUND, AND THIS POWER ALLOWS A SENTENCE TO HAVE TWO OR MORE DIFFERENT PREDICATES FOR THE SAME SUBJECT.

SUPER EXAMPLES:

Rat-man grabbed his knife and cut the cheese.

One subject:
Rat-man
**Compound
predicate (two):**

grabbed his knife and cut the cheese

The troubled city begged for protection and cried out for justice.

One subject: The troubled city
Compound predicate (two):

begged for protection and cried out for justice

THE COMPLETION TEAM'S POWER OF COMPLETE SENTENCES!

The Subject and the Predicate have a combined power called the power of Complete Sentences, and this superpower allows the Subject and the Predicate to join forces to form a complete sentence.

Every sentence needs two parts in order to be complete: a **subject** and a **predicate**.

The subject of a sentence is the main character—the person, place, or thing that the predicate is communicating something about.

And the predicate is the part of the sentence that is communicating something about the subject.

Here's an example:

The hero rescued the crowd.

The subject of this sentence is "The hero" because "The hero" is the person, place, or thing that the sentence is communicating something about.

And the predicate of this sentence is "rescued the crowd" because that's the part of the sentence that is communicating something about the subject.

THE POWER OF COMPLETE SENTENCES:

THE SUBJECT AND THE PREDICATE HAVE THE POWER TO JOIN FORCES TO FORM A COMPLETE SENTENCE.

All by themselves, these parts of a sentence don't say much because they're not complete.

The hero

rescued the crowd.

But by using their combined superpower—the power of Complete Sentences—the Subject and the Predicate can join forces.

The hero rescued the crowd.

And with the Subject and the Predicate joined together, this sentence is now complete and correct.

The power of Complete Sentences is a very important superpower because a sentence cannot be correct unless it's complete. Also, whenever the Subject and the Predicate join forces, their combined power acts like a super protective armor that defends your sentences against grammar mistakes, because a *complete sentence* is a strong sentence.

So, citizen, always remember to join forces with the Completion Team and they'll always use their combined power to keep your sentences completely strong and completely correct.

SUPER EXAMPLES:

Double Vision is looking for clues.

Double Vision

The sentence has a subject.

is looking for clues.

It also has a predicate.

Double Vision is looking for clues.

And by joining forces, they form a complete sentence.

The Prickly Pair are causing trouble.

The Prickly Pair

The sentence has a subject.

 are causing trouble.

It also has a predicate.

The Prickly Pair are causing trouble.

And by joining forces, they form a complete sentence.

THE AMAZING EIGHT!

Behold the power of the Amazing Eight! The members of the Amazing Eight are also known as the *parts of speech*—the individual words that make up our sentences—and they use their unique abilities to empower our sentences.

EACH AND EVERY MEMBER OF THIS SUPER-TEAM HAS A SPECIAL FUNCTION WITHIN A SENTENCE, AND TOGETHER THEY COMBINE THEIR ABILITIES TO ENHANCE OUR SENTENCES IN A MULTITUDE OF WAYS.

With the Amazing Eight, we can create sentences about people, places, and things; we can express action, thinking, or being; and we can strengthen our sentences with dynamic qualities, such as description, relationship, and emotion.

In other words, citizen, whatever it is that your sentences need to say, the Amazing Eight will always fight to help them say it!

THE AMAZING EIGHT SUPER-TEAM MEMBERS:

- **THE NOUN TEAM:**
  THE COMMON NOUN AND THE PROPER NOUN
- **THE PRONOUN**
- **THE VERB TEAM:**
  THE VERB AND THE PRIMARY HELPING VERB

- **THE ADJECTIVE**
- **THE ADVERB**
- **THE CONJUNCTION**
- **THE PREPOSITION**
- **THE INTERJECTION**

THE NOUN TEAM!

The members of the Noun Team are a proud and dedicated part of the power-enhanced words known as the Amazing Eight, but even with superpowers, being a noun is a big job. That's why the Noun Team has two dedicated members ready to meet the task: the Common Noun and the Proper Noun.

THESE TWO AMAZING PARTS OF SPEECH ARE A VERY FLEXIBLE PAIR OF SHAPE-SHIFTERS, AND WITH THEIR SUPERPOWERS, THEY CAN BE ANY NUMBER OF PERSONS, PLACES, OR THINGS WITHIN A SENTENCE.

That's right, citizen. Anyone, anywhere, or anything that you want to write about in a sentence is possible because, no matter what it is, these two members of the Noun Team have got your back.

THE NOUN TEAM MEMBERS:

THE COMMON NOUN
THE PROPER NOUN

THE COMMON NOUN!

It's a bird! It's a plane! Either way—it's still a noun. This shape-shifting superhero, the Common Noun, is a member of the team of power-enhanced words known as the Amazing Eight, and this flexible part of speech can transform into any word that is a person, place, or thing within a sentence.

Here are some examples:

That man can fly.
The bank is surrounded.
My cape is stuck.

The nouns in these sentences are: "man," "bank," and "cape." These words are all nouns because each of them is a person, place, or thing:

man is a person
bank is a place
cape is a thing

These nouns are all general descriptions of a person, place, or thing. And whenever nouns are a general description of a person, place, or thing, they're called common nouns.

The Common Noun's super ability to take the form of a word that is a common noun is a huge help to our sentences. Because let's face it, citizen, there are a lot of common nouns out there! And without the Common Noun's ability to be a word that is any common person, place, or thing, our sentences would be very empty.

SUPERPOWER:

THE COMMON NOUN CAN CHANGE HIS FORM TO BE ANY COMMON, OR INFORMAL, PERSON, PLACE, OR THING IN A SENTENCE.

SUPER EXAMPLES:

My home is far away.

home: noun as a place

This safe is burglar proof.

safe: noun as a thing (concrete/tangible)

THE PROPER NOUN!

SUPERPOWER:

THE PROPER NOUN CAN CHANGE INTO A PERSON, PLACE, OR THING THAT HAS A SPECIFIC (PROPER) NAME. THIS MEANS THAT THE PROPER NOUN WILL ALWAYS START WITH A CAPITAL LETTER.

THE PROPER NOUN!

Now, citizen, please allow me to introduce to you a most excellent part of speech and sentence superhero, the Proper Noun.

The Proper Noun has the same shape-changing abilities as his partner, the Common Noun, but the Proper Noun will only use his powers to change into a person, place, or thing that has a specific, or proper, name.

Here are some examples:

Sarah Johnson has mutant powers.
Fort Knox has been robbed.
Martians are strange creatures.

The proper nouns in these sentences are: "Sarah Johnson," "Fort Knox," and "Martians." These words are all proper nouns because each of them is a specific person, place, or thing:

Sarah Johnson is a person
Fort Knox is a place
Martians are things

Proper nouns always start with a capital letter. And since all of these nouns have specific names that start with a capital letter, we can be certain that they are indeed proper nouns.

The Proper Noun's super ability to shape-shift and take the form of any specific person, place, or thing provides a tremendous service to our sentences. Because even though there are a lot of common nouns out there, there are just as many nouns that have formal names and titles. And without the Proper Noun's assistance, our sentences just wouldn't be . . . well, proper.

So, citizen, the next time any of your sentences need a specific person, place, or thing, be sure to call on the most formal of the Noun Team members, the Proper Noun.

SUPER EXAMPLES:

Dr. Brainstorm is hatching an evil plot.

Dr. Brainstorm: a proper noun as a person

Dr. Brainstorm

Friday is doomsday!

Friday: a proper noun as a thing (abstract/ intangible)

Friday

THE PRONOUN!

The Pronoun is the most professional, proactive, and proficient member of the Amazing Eight, and this awesome all-star superhero is here to help regular nouns go pro!

Pronouns are words that have the power to take the place of regular nouns (common or proper) in a sentence. Pronouns do this to help keep our sentences super clean and super efficient.

THE PRONOUN IS A VERY POWERFUL AND USEFUL *PART OF SPEECH*, AND HE IS IN POSSESSION OF SEVERAL AWESOME POWERS.

These awesome powers allow the Pronoun to become several different types of pronouns that are super helpful in several different ways.

And, citizen, once you learn each of these different powers, you'll know the true power of the Pronoun.

POWERS OF THE PRONOUN:

1. THE POWER TO BE PERSONAL
2. THE POWER TO BE REFLEXIVE
3. THE POWER TO BE POSSESSIVE

THE PRONOUN'S POWER TO BE PERSONAL!

The Pronoun has the power to be Personal, or to become a personal pronoun, and this power allows the Pronoun to take the place of a specific noun in a sentence.

Personal pronouns are words—like **I**, **you**, **he**, **she**, **it**, **us**, **them**—and they help us to keep our sentences lean and efficient by taking the place of longer specific nouns.

Here are some examples:

**Cyber-Scorpion is breaking out of jail.
If we don't stop Cyber-Scorpion soon,
Cyber-Scorpion will escape.**

These two sentences above are both talking about, or referring to, Cyber-Scorpion. We know this because both of these sentences include his full name.

But once any specific noun has been established, or referred to, in a sentence or paragraph, any repetition of that same specific noun can then be replaced with a shorter personal pronoun, like this:

**Cyber-Scorpion is breaking out of jail.
If we don't stop him soon, he will escape.**

The personal pronouns in the second sentence, "him" and "he," have the power to take the place of the specific (proper) noun, "Cyber-Scorpion." And we can be sure that these two personal pronouns are referring to the specific noun "Cyber-Scorpion" because "Cyber-Scorpion" was already referred to, in the first sentence.

By simply using any specific noun in a sentence or paragraph just once, you establish it as a noun that can then be replaced by an appropriate personal pronoun. Whenever a specific noun has been established in this way, it is called the *antecedent*.

And because we decided to use a personal pronoun instead of repeating "Cyber-Scorpion" throughout these two sentences, our example is shorter and easier to say.

Personal pronouns can also inform you about four specific qualities:

1) **Number:** Number tells us if a pronoun is singular or plural.

2) **Person:** Person tells us if a pronoun is in the first person, second person, or third person.
   - The first person lets us refer to ourselves in a sentence (I, me, or we).
   - The second person lets us directly address someone (you).
   - The third person lets us refer to somebody indirectly (he, she, it, they).

3) **Gender:** Gender tells us if a pronoun is male (he), female (she), or neutral (it).

4) **Case:** Case tells us if a pronoun is in the subject form (acting as the subject of a sentence) or in the object form (acting as the object of a sentence). Whenever a pronoun, or any noun, within a sentence is not acting as the subject, then it's an object.

SUPERPOWER:

THE POWER TO BE PERSONAL ALLOWS THE PRONOUN TO TAKE THE PLACE OF A SPECIFIC NOUN IN A SENTENCE.

The chart below shows the qualities related to each personal pronoun.

PERSONAL PRONOUNS:

	SINGULAR		PLURAL	
	Subject	Object	Subject	Object
First Person	I	me	we	us
Second Person	you	you	you	you
Third Person	he she it	him her it	they	them

If we use the personal pronoun "he," from the previous example, and we reference the personal pronoun chart, we can see that "he" represents a specific person who is:

Number: singular
Person: third person
Gender: male
Case: subject form

The information about a pronoun's number, person, gender, and case is super useful when it comes to correctly structuring your sentences, so always remember to double-check your pronouns to make sure that they're a correct match for the noun they are replacing.

SUPER EXAMPLES:

Elastic-man is cool. He can stretch like rubber.

antecedent:
Elastic-man
personal pronoun:

He

Mudskipper Mugger, you are a slippery character.

antecedent:
Mudskipper Mugger
personal pronoun:

you

THE PRONOUN'S POWER TO BE REFLEXIVE!

The Pronoun has the power to be Reflexive, or to become a reflexive pronoun, and this power allows the Pronoun to refer back to the subject of the sentence.

Here's an example:

I will destroy you myself.

The reflexive pronoun, "myself," refers back to the subject of the sentence, "I."

Reflexive pronouns are always a reflection of the subject of the sentence, and because of this they must always be linked with a subject. If a reflexive pronoun is ever used as an independent element in a sentence, such as a subject or an object, it will be incorrect.

Here's an example:

My sidekick and myself protect this city.

The reflexive pronoun in this sentence, "myself," is not being used correctly because instead of referring back to a subject, this reflexive pronoun is actually acting as the subject.

The proper type of pronoun to use in this situation is a personal pronoun. Like this:

My sidekick and I protect this city.

The personal pronoun "I" is the best fit for this sentence because "I" is singular, in the first person, and in the subject form.

Now that this sentence has the proper subject forms, we can still add a reflexive pronoun, like this:

My sidekick and I protect this city ourselves.

This reflexive pronoun, "ourselves," is referring back to the plural subjects of this sentence, "My sidekick and I," so this reflexive pronoun is correct.

Reflexive pronouns also have the power to inform you about these specific qualities:

1) **Number:** singular or plural
2) **Person:** first person, second person, or third person
3) **Gender:** male, female, or neutral

Since reflexive pronouns are a reflection of the subject of the sentence, they can only ever have one case: the subject form.

The chart below shows the qualities related to each reflexive pronoun.

REFLEXIVE PRONOUNS:

	SINGULAR		PLURAL	
	Subject	Object	Subject	Object
First Person	myself		ourselves	
Second Person	yourself		yourselves	
Third Person	himself herself itself		themselves	

SUPERPOWER:

THE POWER TO BE REFLEXIVE ALLOWS THE PRONOUN TO REFER BACK TO THE SUBJECT OF THE SENTENCE.

SUPER EXAMPLES:

His arm has regenerated itself.

itself: reflexive pronoun referring back to the subject, "His arm"

She shielded herself from the bullets.

herself: reflexive pronoun referring back to the subject, "She"

THE PRONOUN'S POWER TO BE POSSESSIVE!

The Pronoun has the power to be Possessive, or to become a possessive pronoun, and this power allows the Pronoun to show possession, or ownership, without the use of an apostrophe.

Here's an example:

The death ray is mine.

The possessive pronoun, "mine," tells us that the death ray (noun) is owned.

Possessive pronouns also have the power to inform you about these specific qualities:

1) **Number:** singular or plural
2) **Person:** first person, second person, or third person
3) **Gender:** male, female, or neutral

The chart below shows the qualities related to each possessive pronoun.

POSSESSIVE PRONOUNS:

	SINGULAR	PLURAL
	Subject/Object	Subject/Object
First Person	my, mine	our, ours
Second Person	your, yours	your, yours
Third Person	his her, hers its	their, theirs

SUPERPOWER:

THE POWER TO BE POSSESSIVE ALLOWS THE PRONOUN TO SHOW POSSESSION WITHOUT THE USE OF AN APOSTROPHE.

SUPER EXAMPLES:

The blue plasma blaster is yours.

yours: a (singular/ second person/ object form) pronoun showing possession

The victory is ours.

ours: a (plural/first person/object form) pronoun showing possession

THE VERB TEAM!

THE VERB TEAM MEMBERS:

THE VERB
THE PRIMARY HELPING VERB

THE VERB TEAM!

The Verb Team is a vibrant pair of valiant verbs, and as dedicated members of the Amazing Eight, these parts of speech work to keep our sentences action-packed and super expressive.

The two members that belong to the Verb Team are the Verb and the Primary Helping Verb.

The Verb, sometimes called, the "Main Verb," is the super-charged team leader of the group. She is by far the most powerful member of the Verb Team, and she uses every bit of her electric energy to give our sentences everything that they need to express themselves to the fullest.

The Primary Helping Verb is the Verb's sidekick, and this fearless assistant is always ready to help out with her unique form of energy whenever the Verb needs it.

AS YOU CAN SEE, CITIZEN, THE SUPER ENERGETIC MEMBERS OF THE VERB TEAM ARE CHARGED WITH A SPECIAL KIND OF ELECTRIC ENERGY THAT ONLY VERBS POSSESS, AND ONCE YOU LEARN TO HARNESS THIS AMAZING ENERGY CORRECTLY—THE POWER OF VERBS WILL BE YOURS!

THE VERB!

THE VERB'S POWERS OF EXPRESSION:

1. STATE OF ACTION
2. STATE OF BEING

THE VERB!

Every sentence contains a special kind of word that is supercharged with energy. The energy from this word allows a sentence to stand, run, jump, and fly. It also allows a sentence to think, reason, feel, and dream. This word is what brings a sentence to life. This word—this energy—is the Verb!

As a member of the Amazing Eight, the Verb uses her amazing energy to set your sentences into motion with the power of Expression. This power can be used to express either a *state of action* or a *state of being*.

AND WITH THESE TWO FORMS OF EXPRESSIONS, THE VERB HAS THE AMAZING POWER TO BRING ANY SENTENCE TO LIFE.

SUPERPOWER:

THE VERB HAS THE POWER TO EXPRESS A *STATE OF ACTION* OR A *STATE OF BEING*.

THE VERB'S POWER OF EXPRESSION: STATE OF ACTION!

The Verb has the power to express a *state of action*. This means that verbs can show action, like physical activity and movement.

Here's an example:

The hero captures crooks.

The verb, "captures," expresses an action: the act of capturing.

Without this verb in the sentence, you'd have a hero and a crook, but they wouldn't be doing anything. It's the verb of the sentence that gives the sentence its action.

Whenever verbs express a state of action, they are called action verbs.

SUPERPOWER:

THE VERB HAS THE POWER TO EXPRESS A *STATE OF ACTION*.

SUPER EXAMPLES:

He wrestles wrongdoers.

wrestles: verb expressing a state of action

wrestles

The mutant insects destroy entire cities.

destroy: verb expressing a state of action

destroy

THE VERB'S POWER OF EXPRESSION: STATE OF BEING!

The Verb also has the power to express a *state of being*.

State of being means that, instead of an action, the verb can show a condition of how something is existing in the world. A state of being, or condition of being, is a way for us to communicate how we are, how we're feeling, and how things are behaving around us.

Here's an example:

I am invulnerable.

The verb, "am," expresses a state of being: the condition of being invulnerable.

Everything has a state of being—everything. And thanks to the Verb, everything is able to *express* it.

SUPERPOWER:

THE VERB HAS THE POWER TO EXPRESS A *STATE OF BEING!*

SUPER EXAMPLES:

She feels courageous.

feels: verb expressing a state of being

feels

I believe in heroes.

believe: verb expressing a state of being

believe

THE VERB: ADDITIONAL POWERS!

Aside from bringing a sentence to life with the power of Expression, the Verb also has a few other useful abilities.

These abilities include being able to control her *number* and *person*, and her *tense*.

BY CONTROLLING HER NUMBER AND PERSON, AND HER TENSE, THE VERB IS ABLE TO KEEP OUR SENTENCES SUPER AGREEABLE AND ALSO VERY TIMELY.

SUPERPOWER:

THE VERB HAS THE POWER TO CONTROL THESE QUALITIES:
- NUMBER AND PERSON
- TENSE

THE VERB'S POWER TO CONTROL NUMBER AND PERSON!

The Verb has the power to control these two specific qualities: number and person.

Number: Number tells us if a verb is in the singular form or in the plural form.

Person: Person tells us if a verb is in the first person, second person, or third person.

- The first person lets us refer to ourselves in a sentence (I am; we are)
- The second person lets us refer to a second person (you are)
- The third person lets us refer to a third person (he is; she is; we are)

Having the ability to control her number and person is very important because in order for a sentence to be correct, the Verb and the Subject must both match, or agree on, their number and person.

WITH THESE POWERS, THE VERB CAN SHIFT HER NUMBER AND PERSON SO THAT THEY CAN ALWAYS AGREE WITH THE NUMBER AND PERSON OF THE SUBJECT.

Here's an example:

I am invincible.

The verb, "am," is singular in number and in the first person so that it can agree with the subject, "I," which is also singular in number and in the first person.

The chart below shows the different forms of the verb "to be" and their matching subject forms.

THE VERB: TO BE

	SINGULAR		PLURAL	
	Subject	Verb	Subject	Verb
First Person	I	am	we	are
Second Person	you	are	you	are
Third Person	he/she/it	is	they	are

SUPERPOWER:

THE VERB HAS THE POWER TO CONTROL *NUMBER* AND *PERSON* TO AGREE WITH THE SUBJECT.

SUPER EXAMPLES:

I am a lawbreaker.

am: singular/first person

They are superheroes.

are: plural/second person

THE VERB'S POWER TO CONTROL TENSE!

The Verb has the power to control the *tense* (location in time) of a sentence. This ability is like having the power of time travel, and the Verb is the only part of speech with the power it takes to control the tense of a sentence.

With this amazing power, the Verb can set a sentence in the present, past, or future.

Here are some examples:

I defend justice.
I defended justice.
I will defend justice.

The verb in each sentence controls the tense. As the verb changes its tense, the tense of the sentence changes with it:

defend   **(present)**
defended   **(past)**
will defend   **(future)**

The Verb has the power to switch into the *present* or *past* tense without any assistance, but in order to create the *future* tense, the Verb must have the assistance of her sidekick, the Primary Helping Verb.

The future tense is created by placing the primary helping verb "will" before any verb that is set in the present tense (will + verb).

SUPERPOWER:

THE VERB HAS THE POWER TO CONTROL THE *TENSE* OF A SENTENCE.

The Verb also has the power to control which *form* of verb tense a sentence can take. There are four forms of verb tenses, and they are:

1) **Simple:** The action is in the present, past, or future.

2) **Progressive:** The action is in progress in the present, past, or future.

3) **Perfect:** The action has been completed in the present, past, or future.

4) **Perfect Progressive:** The action has started and is in progress in the present, past, or future.

The chart below shows the four forms of verb tenses for the verb "defend."

FORMS OF TENSES:

	SIMPLE	PROGRESSIVE be+verb+ing	PERFECT have+verb+ed	PERFECT PROGRESSIVE have+been+verb+ed
PRESENT	defend	am defending	have defended	have been defending
PAST	defended	was defending	had defended	had been defending
FUTURE will + verb	will defend	will be defending	will have defended	will have been defending

The Verb has the power to switch into the *simple present* and the *simple past* tense without any assistance, but in order to create a tense form that is in the *progressive, perfect,* or *perfect progressive,* the Verb must have the assistance of her sidekick and friend, the Primary Helping Verb.

SUPER EXAMPLES:

I am all-powerful.

am: present tense

I was all-powerful.

was: past tense

I will be all-powerful.

will be: future tense

THE PRIMARY HELPING VERB!

SUPERPOWER:

THE PRIMARY HELPING VERB HAS THE POWER TO HELP THE VERB CREATE COMPLEX TENSES, CREATE POSITIVE AND NEGATIVE STATEMENTS, AND ASK QUESTIONS.

The Primary Helping Verb is a faithful sidekick to the Verb, and she is always ready to help the Verb to perform complex tasks.

One of the tasks that the Primary Helping Verb assists the Verb with is creating different tenses. Together they can create the future tense and other (complex) tense forms: progressive, perfect, and perfect progressive (see pages 69–70).

Here's an example:

I will break the law.

The main verb of this sentence, "break," combined with the helping verb, "will," is able to switch the tense of this sentence from the present into the future. Without the helping verb, "will," the sentence would have remained in the present tense.

When creating complex verb tenses, such as the *future perfect progressive*, a sentence can include as many as three primary helping verbs, like this:

As of tomorrow, I will have been fighting crime for fifteen years.

The main verb of this sentence, "fighting," needs all three primary helping verbs, "will have been," to help it change into the future perfect progressive tense.

Without the addition of all three of these helping verbs, "will have been," this sentence would not have been able to create this complex verb tense.

Another task that the Primary Helping Verb assists the Verb with is creating positive statements, negative statements, and questions.

Here's an example:

I do uphold the law.

The main verb of this sentence, "uphold," is being assisted by the primary helping verb, "do," to help it create a positive statement.

With the addition of the helping verb, "do," this sentence was able to create a positive statement.

Without the aid of the helping verb, the sentence would only be able to make a basic, neutral statement.

The chart below is a list of primary helping verbs and how they're used to help the main verb of a sentence.

PRIMARY HELPING VERBS

Help to create different verb tenses	be, am, are, is, been, being, was, were, has, had, have
Help to create positive statements, negative statements, and questions	did, do, does

SUPER EXAMPLES:

I have been absorbing your strength.

have been: helping the main verb (absorbing) show the *present perfect progressive tense.*

have been

Does she know my secret identity?

Does: helping the main verb (know) ask a question.

Does

THE ADJECTIVE!

SUPERPOWER:

THE ADJECTIVE HAS THE ABILITY TO MODIFY NOUNS AND PRONOUNS IN A SENTENCE WITH THE ADDITION OF DESCRIPTIVE DETAIL.

The Adjective is a hero with an incredible eye for detail. And as a member of the Amazing Eight, this hero puts his keen powers of observation to work for the good of all our sentences.

The Adjective is a *modifier*, and with the help of his super handy modifying tool, he delivers a fistful of descriptive power to nouns and pronouns.

The details added by the Adjective serve our sentences by adding richness and interest to the people and objects within them.

Here are some examples:

"The hero" can become "The fearless hero"
"The villain" can become "The twisted villain"

By adding the adjectives "fearless" and "twisted" we've modified these two nouns ("the hero" and "the villain") with descriptive details.

Also, adjectives can be very useful additions to our sentences because they add clarity and understanding by answering questions like:

Which one?
How many?
What kind?

So, the next time you want to add some distinct and dynamic description to your sentences, remember our detail-oriented hero—the Adjective!

SUPER EXAMPLES:

The slimy thief got away.

slimy: adjective answering the question "*Which one of the thieves?*"

slimy

Three heroes are on patrol.

Three: adjective answering the question "*How many heroes?*"

three

THE ADJECTIVE'S POWER OF PHRASING!

The Adjective has the power of Phrasing. Sometimes an adjective needs to be more than a single word to properly do its job. This is when the Adjective uses the power of Phrasing.

This power allows the adjective to stretch out into being several words that act as a single unit within a sentence. This group of words is called a *phrase*, or in this case, an *adjectival phrase*.

SUPER EXAMPLE:

Having twice as many arms can be useful.

twice as many: adjectival phrase answering the question "*How many arms?*"

twice as many

SUPERPOWER:

THE ADJECTIVE HAS THE POWER TO STRETCH OUT INTO BEING SEVERAL WORDS THAT ACT AS A SINGLE UNIT WITHIN A SENTENCE, A *PHRASE*.

THE ADVERB!

SUPERPOWER:

THE ADVERB HAS THE POWER TO MODIFY *VERBS*, *ADJECTIVES*, AND OTHER *ADVERBS* IN A SENTENCE WITH DESCRIPTION.

The Verb—as powerful as she is—can only express so much information before she reaches her limit. That's when the Verb needs a courageous teammate to lend her a helping hand; that's when the Verb needs the the Adverb!

The Adverb is a modifier, and as a valued member of the Amazing Eight, she uses her super handy modifying tool to help give verbs the extra punch that they need to power up a sentence. She does this by adding descriptive information about the specific verb she's modifying.

Here's an example:

I fight.

The verb in this sentence, "fight," can only tell you one thing: I fight. But with the help of an adverb modifying that verb, it can tell you *when*, *where*, *why*, and *how* I fight:

I fight **now**.
I fight **here**.
I fight **for justice**.
I fight **diligently**.

By adding these adverbs, "now," "here," "for justice," and "diligently," we've modified the verb of each sentence ("fight") with useful descriptive information.

The Adverb's modifying abilities make her a powerful ally to the Verb, but this superheroine doesn't stop there. The Adverb also uses her powers to modify adjectives and other adverbs in a sentence. Now that's what I call super teamwork!

So, citizen, if our super friends, the Verb or the Adjective, are ever in need of reinforcements, you now know that the Adverb has got their backs!

SUPER EXAMPLES:

My radioactive body always glows.

always: adverb modifying a verb (glowing *when?*)

always

My enemy attacked surprisingly fast.

surprisingly: verb modifying another adverb (*how fast?*)

surprisingly

THE ADVERB'S POWER OF PHRASING!

The Adverb has the power of Phrasing. Sometimes an adverb needs to be more than a single word to properly do its job. This is when the Adverb uses the power of Phrasing.

This power allows the adverb to stretch out into being several words that act as a single unit within a sentence. This group of words is called a *phrase*, or in this case, an *adverbial phrase*.

SUPER EXAMPLE:

The girl vanished before my eyes.

before my eyes:
adverbial phrase modifying a verb (*vanished where?*)

before my eyes

SUPERPOWER:

THE ADVERB HAS THE POWER TO STRETCH OUT INTO BEING SEVERAL WORDS THAT ACT AS A SINGLE UNIT WITHIN A SENTENCE, A *PHRASE*.

THE CONJUNCTION!

SUPERPOWER:

THE CONJUNCTION HAS THE POWER TO CREATE A CONNECTION BETWEEN WORDS, PHRASES, AND CLAUSES.

It's time to join forces with a heavy-duty connection. He's the Conjunction, and as a member of the Amazing Eight, he has the power to create strong connections, or junctions, between words, phrases, and *clauses*.

Conjunctions are linking words, like **or**, **but**, and **so**, which can be used to make a connection between words, phrases, and clauses. Words, phrases, and clauses often need to join together in many ways and for many different reasons. But whatever the reason for their union, the Conjunction has the power to link them together.

The Conjunction has three different superpowers, and these three powers help him to create three different types of connections. These powers are: Coordination, Correlation, and Subordination.

As you might expect, citizen, each of the Conjunction's connective powers work in a different way, but there is one thing about them you can be sure is always the same—they're all as strong as steel.

POWERS OF THE CONJUNCTION:

1. THE POWER OF COORDINATION
2. THE POWER OF CORRELATION
3. THE POWER OF SUBORDINATION

THE CONJUNCTION'S POWER OF COORDINATION!

The Conjunction has the power of Coordination. This power allows the Conjunction to create a connection between words, phrases, and clauses that are of equal rank, or equal importance.

Here's an example:

I fight crime and tyranny.

The coordinating conjunction, "and," creates a coordinated connection between the words "crime" and "tyranny." This connection shows that these two words are of equal rank in the sentence.

Coordinating conjunctions are the easiest type of conjunction to remember because there are only seven in total, and they're all single words.

The seven coordinating conjunctions are: **and, but, or, so, for, nor,** and **yet.**

SUPERPOWER:

THE CONJUNCTION USES HIS POWER OF COORDINATION TO CREATE CONNECTIONS BETWEEN WORDS, PHRASES, AND CLAUSES THAT ARE OF EQUAL RANK AND IMPORTANCE.

SUPER EXAMPLES:

I stand for truth and justice.

and: coordinating conjunction joining two words of equal rank

You are immensely powerful but just as clumsy.

but: coordinating conjunction joining two phrases of equal rank

THE CONJUNCTION'S POWER OF COORDINATION: JOINING INDEPENDENT CLAUSES!

A *clause* is a section of a sentence. All sentence clauses always include both a subject and a predicate. Sentence clauses can either stand alone, or they can sometimes be properly connected together to form longer sentences.

There are two types of sentence clauses:

1) The Independent Clause:
An independent clause is a section of sentence that contains both a subject and a predicate. Independent clauses have the power to stand alone as a complete sentence.

2) The Dependent Clause:
A dependent clause is also a section of sentence that contains both a subject and a predicate, but it also contains a subordinating conjunction. Dependent clauses do not have the power to stand alone as a complete sentence because whenever a subordinating conjunction is part of a sentence clause, that clause then becomes a subordinate, or a dependent, to a stronger independent clause, which means that they must be connected.

The coordinating conjunctions—**and, but, or, so, for, nor,** and **yet**—can also be used to connect together two or more independent clauses (complete sentences) that are of equal rank, but these connections can only be made with the help of the Conjunction's punctuation ally from the Super Symbols team, the Comma.

Here's an example:

She walked right through me,
and I didn't feel a thing.

The combination of the comma (,) and coordinating conjunction, "and," are connecting the first independent clause, "She walked right through me," to the second independent clause, "I didn't feel a thing."

Neither the comma nor the coordinating conjunction "and" is strong enough to join these two independent clauses on their own, but together, they get the job done with ease.

The Conjunction is a powerful superhero, but even he needs the power of proper punctuation to help him make a connection that joins together two or more independent clauses. Luckily, though, the Comma is always ready to join forces with the Conjunction in order to form a strong and correct sentence connection.

COMBINED SUPERPOWER:

BY JOINING FORCES, THE CONJUNCTION AND THE COMMA HAVE THE POWER TO CORRECTLY CONNECT TWO OR MORE INDEPENDENT CLAUSES INTO ONE SOLID SENTENCE.

SUPER EXAMPLES:

You win this battle, but we'll meet again.

, but: a comma and a coordinating conjunction joining two independent clauses

I struck him with all my might, yet he still stands.

, yet: a comma and a coordinating conjunction joining two independent clauses

THE CONJUNCTION'S POWER OF SUBORDINATION!

The Conjunction has the power of Subordination. This power allows the Conjunction to connect a subordinate (or dependent) clause to a main (or independent) clause.

In this arrangement, the two clauses are not of equal rank. The clause containing the subordinating conjunction becomes a dependent to the stronger main clause.

Here's an example:

I will not rest until justice is served.

The subordinating conjunction, "until," creates a connection between the first independent clause, "I will not rest," and the second dependent clause, "until justice is served."

A subordinate clause that is placed after (or following) a main clause (like in the example above) does not require any extra punctuation.

Subordinating conjunctions can be one, two, or three words long.

SUPER LIST: SUBORDINATING CONJUNCTIONS:

after	before	provided that	unless
although	even if	rather than	when
as	even though	since	whenever
as if	if	so that	where
as long as	if only	supposing	whereas
as much as	in order that	than	wherever
as soon as	lest	that	while
as though	now that	though	why
because	once	till	

SUPERPOWER:

THE CONJUNCTION USES HIS POWER OF SUBORDINATION TO CONNECT A SUBORDINATE CLAUSE TO AN INDEPENDENT CLAUSE.

SUPER EXAMPLES:

You won't be laughing after I capture you.

after: subordinate conjunction that is connecting the subordinate clause ("after I capture you") to a leading main clause ("You won't be laughing")

after

You can't move because you're frozen in ice.

because: subordinate conjunction that is connecting the subordinate clause ("because you're frozen in ice") to a leading main clause ("You can't move")

because

THE CONJUNCTION'S POWER OF SUBORDINATION: JOINING SUBORDINATE CLAUSES!

Even though the Conjunction has the power to join clauses, if it's a subordinate clause that is placed before (or leading) the main clause, then the Conjunction can't do it all by himself. He needs the help of his ally, the Comma.

A subordinate clause can be placed before a main clause, but only with the help of a comma.

Here's an example:

Until justice is served, I will not rest.

Whenever a dependent clause, "Until justice is served," leads an independent clause, "I will not rest," there must also be a comma placed between the two clauses in order to correctly complete the connection.

The combination of a conjunction and proper punctuation allows a leading subordinate clause to be linked to an independent clause.

SUPERPOWER:

THE CONJUNCTION AND THE COMMA HAVE THE POWER TO CORRECTLY CONNECT A LEADING SUBORDINATE CLAUSE TO ITS MAIN CLAUSE.

SUPER EXAMPLES:

If you don't drop your weapon, I'll clobber you.

IF: subordinate conjunction that is connecting a leading subordinate clause ("IF you don't drop your weapon") to a main clause ("I'll clobber you")

Wherever you hide, I'll find you.

Wherever: subordinate conjunction that is connecting a leading subordinate clause ("Wherever you hide") to a main clause ("I'll find you")

Wherever

THE PREPOSITION!

SUPERPOWER:

THE PREPOSITION HAS THE POWER TO SHOW RELATIONSHIPS BETWEEN PEOPLE, PLACES, AND THINGS IN A SENTENCE.

THE PREPOSITION!

This superheroine is ready to travel to great lengths to help your sentences. She's the Preposition, and as a member of the Amazing Eight, she's always *prepped* and ready to help your sentences talk about position.

Prepositions are words—such as **in**, **at**, **by**, **above**, **below**—that allow our sentences to show relationships, or positions, between people, places, and things in a sentence. By showing these relationships, they empower our sentences to show location, time, and direction.

Here's an example:

The bomb exploded on the roof.

The preposition "on" helps us show the relationship between the exploding bomb and the roof. This relationship allows our sentence to show the exploding bomb's location.

Location, *time*, and *direction* are the most common types of relationships that the Preposition is known for creating, but the Preposition can also show relationships involving: possession, responsibility, agency, exclusion, and similarity.

So, citizen, be sure to stay prepped to show your position with the Preposition, because if your sentences ever need to show a location, time, or direction, our hero will always help them go the distance!

PREPOSITIONS SHOW RELATIONSHIPS INVOLVING:

• Location	(at, in, on, above, beside, below, . . .)
• Time	(since, during, until, from, within, . . .)
• Direction	(to, toward, down, past, around, . . .)
• Possession	(of, with)
• Responsibility	(for)
• Agency	(by)
• Exclusion	(except, without)
• Similarity	(as, like, of)

SUPER EXAMPLES:

We fight crime at night.

at: preposition showing time

He has a fist like a rock.

like: preposition showing similarity

THE PREPOSITION'S POWER OF PHRASING!

The Preposition has the power of Phrasing. Sometimes a part of speech needs to be more than a single word to properly do its job. This is when the Preposition uses the power of Phrasing.

This power allows the Preposition to stretch out into several words that act as a single unit. This group of words is called a *phrase*, or in this case, a *prepositional phrase*.

Whenever the Preposition uses her powers she always creates a prepositional phrase. So whenever you find a preposition in a sentence, you'll also find a prepositional phrase.

SUPER EXAMPLE:

You are responsible for my mutation.

For my mutation: prepostional phrase

for my mutation

SUPERPOWER:

THE PREPOSITION HAS THE POWER TO STRETCH OUT INTO BEING SEVERAL WORDS THAT ACT AS A SINGLE UNIT WITHIN A SENTENCE, A *PHRASE*.

THE INTERJECTION!

THE INTERJECTION!

Holy smokes! It's the Interjection—and this sensational superhero is here to make a powerful impact on your sentences!

The Interjection is a prominent member of the Amazing Eight, and he has the power to interject, or insert, a word or expression that adds excitement or emotion to a sentence.

Here's an example:

Wow, you can fly.

In this sentence, the interjection "Wow" adds a burst of excitement to the beginning of the sentence.

Without the interjection, this is only a plain statement: You can fly.

But with the Interjection leading the way, "Wow," the intended excitement and emotion of this sentence is clearly expressed.

Interjections have two different levels of intensity: mild or strong. And the level of intensity is determined by the punctuation used with the interjection.

SUPERPOWER:

THE INTERJECTION HAS THE POWER TO INTERJECT EXCITEMENT OR EMOTION TO THE BEGINNING OF A SENTENCE.

Mild interjections are punctuated with a comma, like this:

Hey, it's the cops.

A comma (,) follows the interjection, "Hey," and connects it to the rest of the sentence.

Strong interjections are punctuated with an exclamation point, like this:

Hey! It's the cops.

With strong interjections, an exclamation point (!) follows the interjection, "Hey," giving it higher intensity and stronger emphasis.

However, exclamation points are sentence-ending punctuation marks (see pg. 112), so, unlike commas, they do not connect their interjections to the rest of the sentence. Instead, interjections followed by exclamation points stand alone as their own separate sentence.

For additional emphasis, exclamation points can also be used to end a sentence that starts with either type of interjection:

Hey, it's the cops!
Hey! It's the cops!

Most interjections are single words, like **hey**, **wow**, **ah**, **oh**, **yeah**.

However, they can also be longer expressions, like these:

Holy Toledo!
Great horny toads!
By Odin's beard!

But whether they're a single word or a longer expression, interjections always add a greater level of excitement or emotional impact to the sentences they're attached to.

So, citizen, the next time your sentence needs to start off with a bang, which part of speech are you going to call into action? Bingo! Call on this superhero—the Interjection!

SUPER EXAMPLES:

Yuck, you're super sticky.

Yuck: interjection showing mild excitement or emotion

Yuck

Great Scott! They're in danger.

Great Scott!: interjection showing strong excitement or emotion

Great Scott!

THE SUPER SYMBOLS!

Never—ever—underestimate the power of punctuation! They may be small, and they may not be words, but they have a lot to say in your sentences.

THE MEMBERS OF THE SUPER SYMBOLS ARE ALSO KNOWN AS *PUNCTUATION MARKS*, AND THEY ARE DEDICATED TO BRINGING SOLID STRUCTURE AND ORDER TO ALL OF YOUR SENTENCES.

Each punctuation mark has a specific power, and the only way to unlock this power is by learning their specific symbol. But once you've mastered their code, citizen, the Super Symbols of punctuation will forever fight to keep your sentences bulletproof.

SUPER SYMBOL SUPER-TEAM MEMBERS:

- THE PERIOD
- THE QUESTION MARK
- THE EXCLAMATION POINT
- THE COMMA
- THE APOSTROPHE
- THE COLON

- THE SEMICOLON
- THE HYPHEN
- THE DASH
- THE PARENTHESES
- THE QUOTATION MARKS
- THE ELLIPSIS

THE PERIOD!

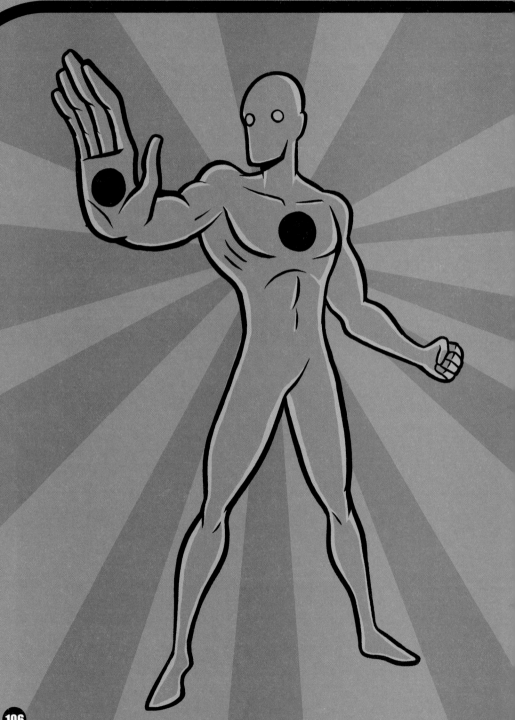

Although the Period is one of the smallest symbols that you'll ever see in a sentence, this pint-sized punctuation can stop any sentence of any size without ever breaking a sweat.

Here's an example:

The supervillain is unstoppable.

The supervillain in this sentence may not be stoppable, but this sentence is. In fact, we know this sentence has stopped because it has a period (.) at the end of it.

A period is a sentence-ending punctuation mark and a clear signal that the sentence has come to a full stop.

Signaling the end of a sentence is a very important function, because without periods to signal the full stop of a sentence, we wouldn't know where one sentence ended and where another began, and that would be a super confusing mess.

The Period is by far the most used of all the sentence-ending punctuation marks, and with good reason. This sentence terminator gets his job done with no fuss, no grandstanding, and with no questions asked. And you can also be sure that no matter how short, lengthy, or ridiculously long a sentence is, the Period can make it stop.

So, citizen, now you know that if you see this Super Symbol at the end of a sentence, that sentence, no matter its length, has undoubtedly come to an end—period.

SUPERPOWER:

THE PERIOD HAS THE POWER TO SIGNAL THE END OF A SENTENCE. HE CAN STOP ANY SENTENCE OF ANY SIZE, AND HE LETS THE READER KNOW THAT THE SENTENCE HAS COME TO A FULL STOP.

SUPER EXAMPLES:

I'll stop him.

The Period can end very short sentences.

I'll stop him from breaking the law, and I'll bring him to justice because it's my sworn (and self-imposed) duty to stand against tyranny, but first I'm going to need a bowling ball, two banana peels, and a net.

The Period can end very long (and sometimes silly) sentences, too.

THE QUESTION MARK!

SUPERPOWER:

THE QUESTION MARK HAS THE POWER TO TURN ANY SENTENCE INTO A QUESTION.

THE QUESTION MARK!

Are you looking for answers, citizen? If so, the Question Mark is on your side.

The Question Mark is a very curious superhero, and this inquisitive piece of punctuation constantly seeks the answers to all of life's questions, big and small. And as a member of the Super Symbols, the Question Mark gets these answers by using his super curiosity to turn any sentence into a question.

Here's an example:

What is your superpower?

The question mark (?) at the end of this sentence signals that this sentence is a question.

Asking questions is greatly important, and question marks allow our sentences to very clearly signal that a question is being asked.

Thanks to the sentence-ending superhero the Question Mark, we have the power to ask any of these questions:

Who, what, where, when, and why?
Which one, how many, and for how long?
Would we, could we, should we, have we?

All of these questions and a whole lot more are possible because of this knowledge-seeking superhero, the Question Mark.

So, citizen, if you're looking for answers, you should definitely team up with this investigative and interrogative superhero, because the Question Mark has the perfect power to help you find them.

SUPER EXAMPLES:

Are you ready for a world of hurt?

?: a sentence ending as a question

Who dropped the stink bomb?

?: a sentence ending as a question

THE EXCLAMATION POINT!

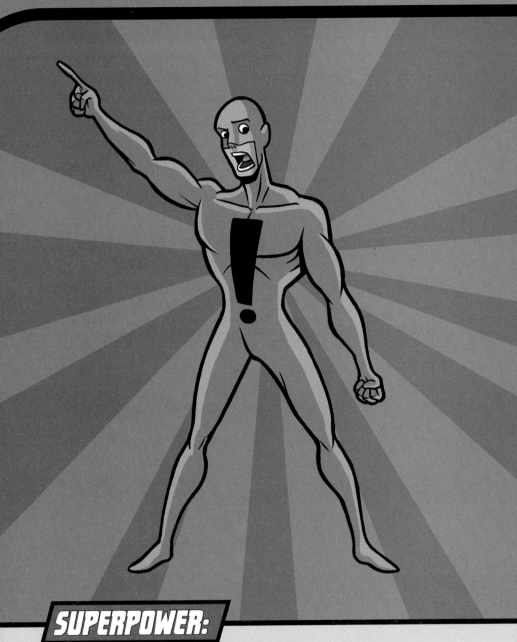

SUPERPOWER:

THE EXCLAMATION POINT IS THE STRONGEST MEMBER OF THE SENTENCE-ENDING TEAM, AND HE HAS THE POWER TO GIVE A SENTENCE STRONG EMOTION AND STRONG EMPHASIS.

From time to time, we all need a sentence that can really stand out and be noticed, and there is only one member of the Super Symbols with the punctuation power to give an entire sentence this kind of extraordinary emphasis. This bold hero of intensity is the Exclamation Point!

The Exclamation Point is the strongest, and loudest, punctuation mark that can be used to end a sentence. When you see him, it means that the sentence you're reading has something very important, very emotional, or very urgent to say.

Here's an example:

We are under attack!

The exclamation point (!) at the end of this sentence signals that it has ended with great emphasis.

It's important for us to know when sentences are being emphasized. Exclamation points are tall, noticeable sentence-ending punctuation symbols that show emphasis, and they are a clear signal of importance, emotion, or urgency.

Exclamation points can also mean that you've "turned up the volume" on a sentence, so it can be used to show that someone is yelling, shouting, or screaming. Like this:

"Run for your life!" she shouted.

Back to the point, the Exclamation Point is simply the perfect punctuation mark to use when you need an important sentence to stand out and be noticed, because this sentence terminator is a superhero who commands your attention, demands your respect, and refuses to be ignored.

So remember, citizen, the next time you need to end a sentence with power and emphasis—call on the Exclamation Point!

SUPER EXAMPLES:

I am master of this planet!

!: for emphasis

I hate giant spiders!

!: for emotion

THE COMMA!

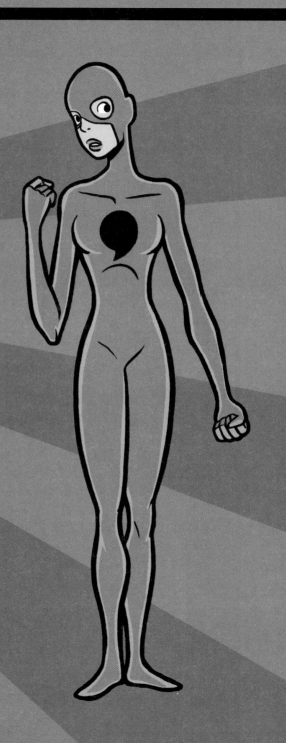

THE COMMA!

Let us pause to appreciate one of the most useful, versatile, and nimble members of the Super Symbols, the Comma.

The Comma can appear several times in the same sentence, performing many different functions that help give that sentence greater structure, stability, and clarity.

Her array of useful powers includes: the power to List a Series, the power to List Multiple Adjectives, and the power to Address.

The Comma has other powers as well. As we saw earlier, she has the ability to join together subordinate and independent clauses with the help of a member of the Amazing Eight, the Conjunction (see pg. 84).

But whether she is using her own special powers, or joining forces with one of her allies, the Comma is always fighting for the good of your sentences, and she always will.

So, citizen, don't let this quiet little punctuation symbol fool you, because the Comma, quite simply, is a powerful force.

POWERS OF THE COMMA:

1. POWER TO LIST A SERIES
2. POWER TO LIST MULTIPLE ADJECTIVES
3. POWER TO ADDRESS
4. POWER OF JOINING SENTENCES (SEE: THE CONJUNCTION)

THE COMMA'S POWER TO LIST A SERIES!

The Comma has the power to List a Series. This power allows the Comma to multiply into several commas that can be used to separate a list of items (either words or groups of words) that occur in a series.

Here's an example:

The crook took the girl's wallet, watch, and jewelry.

The "wallet", "watch", and "jewelry" are each separate items in a list. By placing a comma in between the individual items, we can clearly view each one as a separate and equal addition to the same list.

Whenever there is a list of items in a sentence, they can be separated by commas to show that each separate item is acting as an equal component of the same list. When commas are used in this way, they are often called *serial commas*.

The power to List a Series is essential to keeping the lists in our sentences super organized and properly prioritized.

So, citizen, always be sure to keep the Comma on your list of useful, versatile, and efficient sentence superheroes, and she'll make sure that your lists are always super organized and properly punctuated.

SUPERPOWER:

THE POWER TO LIST A SERIES GIVES THE COMMA THE ABILITY TO SEPARATE A LIST OF ITEMS THAT OCCUR IN A SERIES.

SUPER EXAMPLES:

My powers give me strength, speed, and X-ray vision.

COMMAS: to separate three or more items in a series

Cameras, alarms, and sensors are included in our security system.

COMMAS: to separate three or more items in a series

THE COMMA'S POWER TO LIST MULTIPLE ADJECTIVES!

The Comma has the power to List Multiple Adjectives, and this power gives her the ability to separate multiple adjectives that are modifying the same noun.

Here's an example:

The enormous, metallic, shiny robot is my sidekick.

The words "enormous" and "metallic" and "shiny" can all be separated by commas because they are multiple adjectives that are modifying the same word: "robot."

Nouns can be described, or modified, with more than one adjective. Multiple adjectives can be separated by commas and this shows that each multiple adjective is acting as a separate modifier for the same word.

So, citizen, make sure your multiple modifiers stay on point with our powerful, amazing heroine, the Comma.

SUPERPOWER:

THE POWER TO LIST MULTIPLE ADJECTIVES GIVES THE COMMA THE ABILITY TO SEPARATE MULTIPLE ADJECTIVES THAT ARE MODIFYING THE SAME NOUN.

SUPER EXAMPLES:

Do not press that large, ominous button.

COMMA: separating multiple adjectives that are modifying the same noun

This hairy, smelly, drooling creature is my friend.

COMMA: separating multiple adjectives that are modifying the same noun

THE COMMA'S POWER TO ADDRESS!

The Comma has the power to Address, and this power gives her the ability to directly address a person or group of people in a sentence.

Here's an example:

Captain Hijinks, you are my hero.

This sentence is directly addressing a person: Captain Hijinks. The comma sets Captain Hijinks apart from the rest of the sentence, and that shows us that he's the person being directly addressed.

Any time a sentence is directly addressing a person or group of people, that person or group of people needs to be set apart from the rest of the sentence with a comma. Also, direct addresses can be placed at the beginning, middle, or end of a sentence.

Here are some examples:

Beginning: **Captain Hijinks, you are my hero.**
Middle: **You, Captain Hijinks, are my hero.**
End: **You are my hero, Captain Hijinks.**

But whether a direct address happens at the beginning, middle, or end of a sentence, the person or group of people being addressed must always be identified, and the proper way to do this is by using commas to set them apart from the rest of the sentence.

If a person being addressed in a sentence is not properly set aside with a comma, it can change the meaning of the sentence, and that can cause confusion.

Here's an example:

The evil invaders are dissolving, Captain Hijinks.

This sentence is addressing Captain Hijinks, and it's informing him that the evil invaders are (for some reason) dissolving.

But look what happens if we leave out the comma:

The evil invaders are dissolving Captain Hijinks.

In this sentence, Captain Hijinks is the one being dissolved, by the evil invaders.

Without the comma to set apart Captain Hijinks, he becomes part of the action, which turns out to be very bad news for Captain Hijinks.

SUPERPOWER:

THE POWER TO ADDRESS GIVES THE COMMA THE ABILITY TO DIRECTLY ADDRESS A PERSON OR GROUP OF PEOPLE IN A SENTENCE.

SUPER EXAMPLES:

Dr. Brainstorm, your schemes are always brilliant.

comma: directly addressing a person (at the beginning of a sentence)

People of Earth, surrender your ice cream to us.

comma: directly addressing a group of people (at the beginning of a sentence)

THE APOSTROPHE!

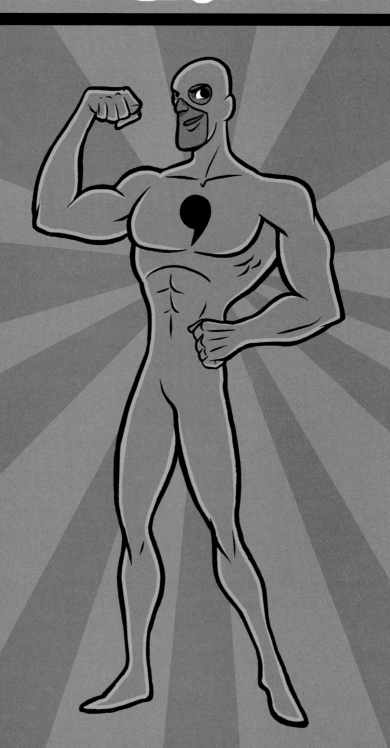

The Apostrophe is a Super Symbols team member who is really packed with power. In fact, this hero has two awesome powers rolled up into his one very amazing punctuation mark.

The Apostrophe's two powers are: the power of Contraction, and the power of Possession. This powerhouse of punctuation uses his first power to help keep our sentences streamlined and efficient, and his second power helps to keep us informed about ownership.

Since the placement of an apostrophe can change the very meaning of a word, the Apostrophe uses a specific set of rules that he diligently follows down to the letter. These rules help him make sure that he's using each of his powers effectively and correctly.

Learn these rules, citizen; commit them to heart; and you too can possess the Apostrophe's amazing punctuation power—times two!

POWERS OF THE APOSTROPHE:

1. THE POWER OF CONTRACTION
2. THE POWER OF POSSESSION

THE APOSTROPHE'S POWER OF CONTRACTION!

The Apostrophe has the power of Contraction. He uses this power to *contract*, or squeeze together, two separate words into one single, shorter, efficient word.

Here's an example:

We will never surrender to you.

The words "We will" can be turned into a contraction, like this:

We'll never surrender to you.

The apostrophe symbol (') shows that the two words, "We will," have been contracted into one word, "We'll," and the apostrophe also represents the letters that are no longer visible after the contraction.

Thanks to the contracting power of the Apostrophe, we can have shorter words that help us keep our sentences lean and polished.

SUPERPOWER:

THE APOSTROPHE HAS THE POWER TO CREATE CONTRACTIONS.

SUPER EXAMPLES:

Where's my grappling hook?

contraction:
Where's = Where is

You shouldn't touch my plutonium.

contraction:
Shouldn't = should not

THE APOSTROPHE'S POWER OF POSSESSION!

The Apostrophe has the power of Possession. He uses this power to allow *single nouns* and *plural nouns* to show possession, or ownership.

Showing possession is an important and useful power because it allows us to show ownership over the things that belong to each of us.

And thanks to the Apostrophe, the ability to have our singular and plural nouns show possession can belong to all of us.

THE APOSTROPHE HAS THE POWER TO SHOW POSSESSION FOR:

1. SINGULAR NOUNS
2. PLURAL NOUNS

THE APOSTROPHE'S POWER OF POSSESSION: SINGULAR NOUNS!

The Apostrophe has the power to show that a singular noun is in the *possessive form* (has possession or ownership).

Here's an example:

The hero's cape is stuck in the door.

The apostrophe followed by a letter **s** at the end of the singular noun "hero" means that this word is showing possession, and this lets us know that the cape belongs to the hero.

To show a singular noun is in the possessive form, add an **'s**.

And, to show that a singular noun that *already* ends with an **s** is in the possessive form, do the same thing: add an **'s**.

SUPERPOWER:

THE APOSTROPHE HAS THE POWER TO SHOW THAT A SINGULAR NOUN IS IN THE POSSESSIVE FORM.

SUPER EXAMPLES:

The creature's breath is horrible.

creature's: a singular noun showing possession

creature's

The boss's plans always work.

boss's: a singular noun (that ends in **s**) showing possession

boss's

THE APOSTROPHE'S POWER OF POSSESSION: PLURAL NOUNS!

The Apostrophe also has the power to show that a plural noun is in the possessive form.

Here's an example:

The invaders' weapons are too powerful.

The apostrophe at the end of the plural noun "invaders" means that this word is showing possession, and this lets us know that the weapons belong to the invaders.

A lot of plural nouns normally end with the letter **s** because it's the letter **s** that is making them plural in the first place.

So, to show the possessive form of these plural nouns, add the apostrophe after the letter **s**, like this: **s'**.

And to show the possessive form for plural nouns that *do not* end in **s**, add **'s**.

SUPERPOWER:

THE APOSTROPHE HAS THE POWER TO SHOW THAT A PLURAL NOUN IS IN THE POSSESSIVE FORM.

SUPER EXAMPLES:

His fists' knuckles are like iron.

fists': a plural noun (that ends in **s**) showing possession

fists'

He is the people's superhero.

people's: a plural noun (not ending in **s**) showing possession

people's

THE COLON!

SUPERPOWER:

THE COLON HAS THE POWER TO SIGNAL AN INTRODUCTION.

THE COLON!

This punctuation mark is the Colon, and as a member of the Super Symbols, he always stands ready to assist your sentences with his power to signal an introduction.

Here's an example:

I fight for one reward: justice.

The colon (:) in this sentence is signaling an introduction. Colons can introduce information that can answer, support, or explain the original sentence. In this case, we learn an answer: The one reward this particular hero fights for is "justice."

The information that follows a colon can start with either a capital letter or with a lowercase letter, whichever is more appropriate. Though keep in mind that in some cases, such as with a quote, a capital letter may be required.

Also, there's one other important rule to keep in mind. The Colon can only signal an introduction for a complete sentence.

In other words, a colon should *never* be used to answer, support, or explain a fragment sentence.

Here's an example:

I fight for: justice.

This sentence is incorrect because the main sentence, "I fight for," is not a complete sentence; it's a weak *fragment*, and a colon can't fix a fragment. So only use a colon if you're certain that it's connected to a complete sentence.

And now, citizen, that you've been properly introduced to the Colon, be sure to call on him whenever your sentences need to signal an introduction for a word, quote, statement, or list.

SUPER EXAMPLES:

I'm not like everyone else: normal.

colon: introducing a word

Only one thing can stop that robot: pulling the plug!

colon: introducing a statement (instructions)

THE SEMICOLON!

SUPERPOWER:

THE SEMICOLON HAS THE POWER TO JOIN TWO OR MORE INDEPENDENT CLAUSES TOGETHER.

The Semicolon is a member of the Super Symbols, and she has the power to join two closely related sentences together. Her style and grace make her an elegant solution to joining two or more closely related sentences, and her ability to single-handedly do the job makes her the obvious and superefficient choice.

Usually, joining two sentences together takes the combined power of the Comma and the Conjunction (see pg. 115 and 184). But when two sentences are so closely related that it almost looks like they belong together, our heroine, the Semicolon, has the power to single-handedly join them together.

Here's an example:

You can't escape; you're surrounded.

The Semicolon (;) elegantly and effectively connects these two closely related sentences into one sentence.

Without the Semicolon, you'd have two separate sentences, each of them ending with a period, like this:

You can't escape. You're surrounded.

The sentences can still work this way, too, but separating the sentences creates an awkward pause. This awkward pause breaks up the power and unity that the sentences once had when they were connected. So it's always a good idea to consider the benefits of using a Semicolon instead.

So now you know, citizen. If you ever need to connect two closely related sentences together, the Semicolon will come to your rescue with style, grace, and power.

SUPER EXAMPLES:

I know you're here; I can sense it.

semicolon: joining two related sentences

You'll pay for this; I swear it.

semicolon: joining two related sentences

THE HYPHEN!

SUPERPOWER:

THE HYPHEN HAS THE POWER TO JOIN TWO OR MORE DIFFERENT WORDS TOGETHER TO ACT AS A NEW SINGLE WORD WITH A COMBINED MEANING.

THE HYPHEN!

All words have the power to communicate their own specific meaning, but sometimes when you need to communicate a larger, more complex meaning, one word alone just won't cut it. That's when you need the power of the Hyphen on your side.

As a member of the Super Symbols, this superhero has the power to join two or more words together into a single, one-of-a-kind, supercharged word.

Here's an example:

That was a death-defying leap!

The hyphen joins together the words "death" and "defying" so that they can act as one word.

Hyphenated words act as one word to communicate a new, combined meaning that the single words can't communicate on their own.

When used separately, neither "death" nor "defying" is able to communicate the same meaning as *death-defying*:

A death leap
A defying leap

It's only after joining the two words together with a hyphen that the new combined meaning can be expressed.

Thanks to the Hyphen's superpower, we can use extraordinary words and expressions like *heart-stopping*, *hand-to-hand*, and *cloak-and-dagger* in our sentences. And being able to use these hyphenated words in our sentences is more than just fun, it's super useful, too.

So, citizen, the next time you need a super one-of-a-kind word with its own special meaning, remember to team up with our word-creating superhero, the Hyphen.

SUPER EXAMPLES:

Her superpowers are mind-numbing!

Mind-numbing: two words that form a new word

mind-numbing

We'll have to fight them back-to-back.

back-to-back: three words that form a new expression

back-to-back

THE DASH!

Usually, punctuation symbols are not meant to be overly flashy, but in the case of this eye-catching heroine—the Dash—flashy is good!

The Dash, however, is more than just glitz and sparkle. She plays a very pivotal and functional role in your sentences by occasionally standing in for her Super Symbols teammates: the Comma, the Semicolon, the Colon, and the Parentheses. The Dash only stands in for them whenever a sentence calls for the extra emphasis that only she can deliver.

Here's an example:

She's the greatest superhero—ever.

The dash (—) is connecting the word "ever" to the rest of the sentence. This type of connection is usually made with a comma, but by choosing to use a dash symbol, the connection is made, and it also adds emphasis.

The Dash's symbol is sometimes called an *em dash* because her symbol is the length of a capital letter M. This long length gives her symbol the super striking character it needs to set off a segment of a sentence with style—and power!

So, citizen, the next time one of your sentences needs to be empowered with a little extra flair and emphasis—remember the Dash.

SUPER EXAMPLES:

His weakness—fire—is my strength.

dash: in place of commas

I will strike—you will fall.

dash: in place of a semicolon

THE PARENTHESES!

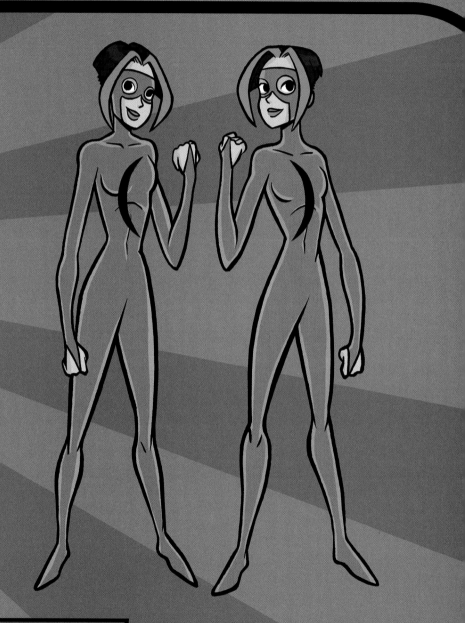

SUPERPOWER:

THE PARENTHESES HAVE THE POWER TO SNEAK SECRET MESSAGES INTO YOUR SENTENCES.

THE PARENTHESES!

As members of the Super Symbols, these stealthy punctuation symbols have the power to sneak secret messages into your unsuspecting sentences. They may appear to be rule breakers, but in actuality, their extra level of concealed communication (when used correctly) only adds to the overall effectiveness of our sentences.

Here's how they work: The first parenthesis "(" shields the front end of the secret message, and the second parenthesis ")" closes off the back end, like this:

(This sentence is a secret message.)

Together, they create a barrier that both hides the secret message away from the rest of the sentence and simultaneously keeps it visible to the reader (that's you). This way, the secret message never interferes with the structure of the sentence, but it still allows the reader to receive the hidden communication.

With their punctuation powers, we can add secret messages of various sizes (including single words, phrases, or entire sentences) to our sentences, and we can add them to various places (such as the beginning, middle, or end) within our sentences.

Just keep in mind, citizen, that the Parentheses are a team, so always keep them paired together. If you don't—you'll totally blow their cover! (And that would stink.)

SUPER EXAMPLES:

I have traveled one light-year (about six trillion miles) to be here.

parenthetical note: adding useful information

You're an evil tyrant! (And you smell bad, too.)

parenthetical note: adding a comment (sometimes, very personal)

THE QUOTATION MARKS!

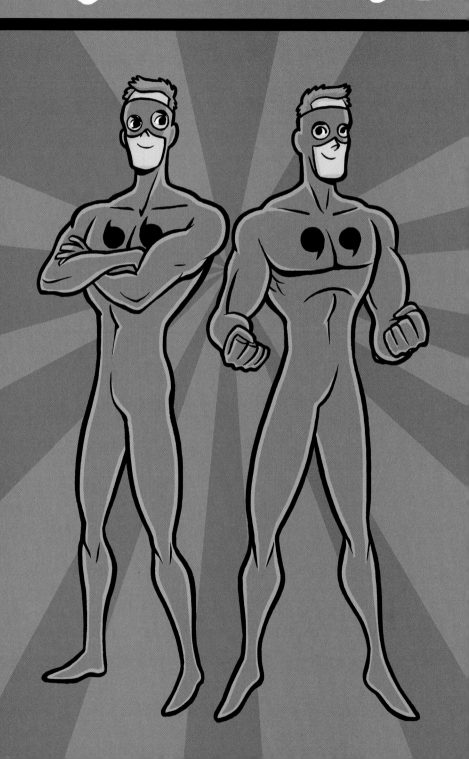

The Quotation Marks are members of the Super Symbols, and as the guardians of direct quotes, these two superheroes are sworn to protect and preserve the *accuracy*, *correctness*, and *integrity* of any quote that is in their care.

Quotation Marks are punctuation symbols that signal the beginning and ending of a direct quote—the words that someone else has written or said.

Here's an example:

The evil villain said, "I will destroy you."

The start quotation mark (") signals the beginning of the quote, and the end quotation mark (") signals the ending of the quote. And, after seeing the quotation marks, we all know, word for word, exactly what the evil villain said: "I will destroy you."

Now keep in mind that when you quote someone, you're responsible for repeating exactly what that person wrote or said—honest and true—and word for word. This is a high standard to live up to, but being honest, truthful, and correct is always something worth fighting for.

And in the end, citizen, if you uphold this high standard of truth when you're making direct quotes, your sentences, your readers, and our truthful twin superheroes, the Quotation Marks, will thank you for it.

SUPERPOWER:

THE QUOTATION MARKS ALLOW US TO REPEAT, OR *QUOTE*, WHAT SOMEONE ELSE HAS WRITTEN OR SAID, WORD FOR WORD.

SUPER EXAMPLES:

Captain Cliché said, "You'll never get away with this."

quotation marks:
signaling a direct quote

"Block the exits," the chief commanded, "and surround the building."

quotation marks:
signaling a direct quote

THE ELLIPSIS!

SUPERPOWER:

THE ELLIPSIS HAS THE POWER TO OMIT WORDS FROM A QUOTE.

THE ELLIPSIS!

The Ellipsis is a member of the Super Symbols, and this helpful heroine knows the power of a good quote. Direct quotes allow us to preserve and pass on valuable information and brilliant ideas. However, some quotes are just way too long to have to repeat word for word, especially if you don't need the whole quote in order to make your point.

Fortunately, the Ellipsis has a very practical superpower, and it allows her to respectfully *omit*, or exclude, unnecessary information from direct quotes.

Here's how it works: Whenever any part of a quote needs to be omitted, or left out, the ellipsis symbol (. . .) takes the place of the omitted material.

Here's an example:

> **"Attention, people of Earth. We come from a distant galaxy. Our brains are large, and our feet look strange. Surrender your planet."**

This quoted statement, even though it's accurate, is a somewhat long statement to repeat. But if we use an ellipsis, we can shorten the overall length of this quote and still keep its intended message, like this:

> **"Attention, people of Earth. . . . Surrender your planet."**

The second quote, with the ellipsis, is much shorter. It delivers the necessary parts of the message without changing the original meaning of the quote. Also, with the ellipsis in place to respectfully represent the missing portion, the integrity of the quote remains intact.

So, citizen, the next time you need to cut your quotes down to size, call on the Ellipsis!

SUPER EXAMPLES:

Entire quote:

"Every superhero knows this by heart. Some argue about who said it first, and others argue about who said it best, but all that matters is that these words are true: With great power comes great responsibility."

—Anonymous superhero

"Every superhero knows this by heart. . . . With great power comes great responsibility."

ellipsis: showing that part of the quote has been omitted.

THE SABOTAGE SQUAD!

e on your guard, citizen, for these scoundrels are the sworn enemies of correct grammar! The Sabotage Squad, also known as grammar mistakes, is a rotten bunch of supervillains who are on an evil mission to destroy all correct sentences.

Each member of the Sabotage Squad is armed with evil powers that can be used to trick, fool, and deceive you into making a grammar mistake, and each one of these outlaws is an expert at wrecking sentences.

SO, CITIZEN, NEVER MAKE THE MISTAKE OF UNDERESTIMATING THE TRICKERY OF THE SABOTAGE SQUAD, BECAUSE WHEN IT COMES TO BREAKING THE RULES OF GRAMMAR— THERE'S NOBODY WORSE.

THE GRAMMAR VILLAINS:

- DOUBLE NEGATIVE
- THE FRAGMENT
- THE RUN-ON
- THE COMMA SPLICE
- THE DISAGREEMENT

DOUBLE NEGATIVE!

EVIL POWER:

DOUBLE NEGATIVE HAS THE POWER TO MAKE YOU SAY THE EXACT OPPOSITE OF WHAT YOU MEAN.

They say that two negatives equal a positive—and this is true—but these two tricksters equal nothing but trouble for your sentences. Double Negative are members of the Sabotage Squad, and these troublesome twins are always trying to trick you into making a gigantic grammar mistake.

One negative word in a sentence is fine, but if Double Negative gets you to use two negative words in the same sentence then they've succeeded in tricking you into saying the exact opposite of what you mean.

Here's an example:

I'm no villain.

This sentence says that I am not a villain. This sentence is clear because it only has one negative word: "no." But watch what happens when we add a second negative word, like this:

I'm not no villain.

This sentence is now saying that I **am** a villain. It might *sound* like this sentence is saying that I'm not a villain, but the second negative word is making the sentence mean the opposite of the first sentence, because, if I'm **not** *no* villain, then I **must be** a villain.

no villain = no villain   not no villain = yes villain

There's a way to strengthen your defenses against double negatives: Learn about negative words. If you learn to recognize and understand negative words, you'll double your protection against double negatives.

So, citizen, if you see two negative words in the same sentence—think twice—because it just might be Double Negative trying to trick you with their double-dealing double talk!

SUPER EXAMPLES:

You're not no superhero.

Double negative: if you're **not no** superhero, then you **must be** a superhero

You're no superhero.

Fixed: by removing the first negative, "not"

You can't never stop me.

Double negative: if you **can't never** stop me, then you **can** stop me

You can't stop me.

Fixed: by removing the second negative, "can't"

THE FRAGMENT!

EVIL POWER:

THE FRAGMENT HAS THE POWER TO FRAGMENT YOUR SENTENCES SO THAT THEY'RE INCOMPLETE AND INCORRECT.

The sentence Fragment is a weak and crumbly bad guy, and as a member of the Sabotage Squad, there's nothing that he enjoys more than breaking up the strength and stability of your sentences. The Fragment does this by fragmenting your sentences so that they're not complete.

Here's an example:

Disappeared into thin air.

This sentence is a fragment because (even though it has a predicate) it's missing a subject.

Without a subject we don't know *what* disappeared into thin air. The only way to fix this broken sentence is by adding a subject, like this:

The thief disappeared into thin air.

By adding a subject, "The thief," the sentence is now complete.

As you saw earlier with the Completion Team, true sentences need both a subject and a predicate in order to be strong and complete (see pg. 32). If a sentence is missing its subject or predicate, then it's not really a complete sentence because it's only half complete, or in other words, it's only a fragment of a sentence.

This cracked supervillain, the Fragment, really loves a fractured sentence, but in the end he is no match for the combined strength of the Completion Team. The Subject and the Predicate are the two superheroes that make up this powerful team, and as long as you keep them teamed up with each other, the Fragment doesn't stand a chance.

So remember, citizen, if you don't want your sentences to crumble and fall apart just like the Fragment does—never let him break up the team!

SUPER EXAMPLES:

The Mole King and his subjects.

Fragment: Missing a predicate (The Mole King and his subjects are doing what?)

The Mole King and his subjects are attacking.

Fixed: by adding a predicate

Eating up the entire city.

Hipposaurus Rex is eating up the entire city.

Fixed: by adding a subject

THE RUN-ON!

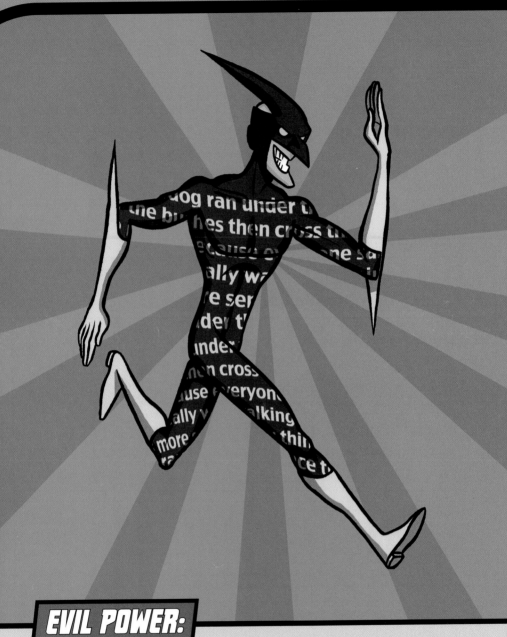

EVIL POWER:

THE RUN-ON MAKES YOUR SENTENCES RUN INTO EACH OTHER WITHOUT ANY PUNCTUATION. AFTER HE'S FINISHED, YOU'LL HAVE EXTRA LONG SENTENCES THAT RUN ON, AND ON, AND ON.

The Run-on is a member of the Sabotage Squad, and this reckless runner is always trying to pull a fast one on your sentences. Complete sentences can't just *run on* into each other to form extended sentences—but that's the problem with the Run-on. This hasty villain makes your first sentence run right past your punctuation and straight into the next sentence.

Here's an example:

I see you I have night vision.

This is a run-on sentence: two complete sentences running into each other without proper punctuation.

Complete sentences must either be ended with proper sentence-ending punctuation, like this:

I see you. I have night vision.

Or they must be properly joined together by using the combination of a comma with a coordinating conjunction or by using a semicolon, whichever is more appropriate. In this case, a semicolon (;) is the better choice:

I see you; I have night vision.

Sometimes sentences need to be long and sometimes sentences need to be short, but long or short, every sentence always needs proper punctuation.

Without proper punctuation, your sentences will all run into each other, and that will only lead to extra long sentences that never seem to stop.

So, citizen, always remember to use the power of punctuation in all of your sentences. If you do that, you'll always be able to stop the Run-on in his tracks!

SUPER EXAMPLES:

I can't fly my powers are gone.

Run-on: two complete sentences running together with no punctuation.

I can't fly; my powers are gone.

Fixed: by adding a semicolon to properly join into one sentence.

You'll never break those chains they're made out of solid titanium even you don't have that kind of strength.

Run-on: three complete sentences running together with no punctuation.

You'll never break those chains. They're made out of solid titanium, and even you don't have that kind of strength.

Fixed: by adding a period to separate the first two sentences, and then adding a comma and a conjunction to properly join the remaining two sentences into one.

THE COMMA SPLICE!

EVIL POWER:

THE COMMA SPLICE HAS THE POWER TO FOOL YOU INTO THINKING THAT SHE CAN JOIN TOGETHER TWO COMPLETE SENTENCES.

Beware, citizen, for this is not really the Comma! This imposter is the Comma Splice, and as a sinister member of the Sabotage Squad, this counterfeit comma is out to fool you into making a classic grammar mistake: splicing together complete sentences.

Real commas are useful and powerful pieces of punctuation, but they don't have the power to join two complete sentences together. That's why true commas would never try to do such a thing. But the Comma Splice is on a mission to trick you into thinking that she has the power to join complete sentences.

Here's an example:

They need help, I must fly to the rescue.

This sentence is not correct. It's a comma splice: a fake comma that is incorrectly *splicing*, or patching, together two complete sentences.

Complete sentences cannot be correctly joined together by a single comma. In order to be joined correctly, complete sentences must either be: 1) ended with proper sentence-ending punctuation, 2) properly joined together by using the combination of a comma with a coordinating conjunction, or 3) joined together using a semicolon.

To fix this sentence, we'll use a semicolon, like this:

They need help; I must fly to the rescue.

So, citizen, now that you know about this counterfeit comma, the Comma Splice, don't let her fool you into splicing your sentences together; because in the end, no matter how you splice it—it's still a mistake!

SUPER EXAMPLES:

I can't believe it, he's breaking loose.

comma splice: two complete sentences spliced together with a comma.

I can't believe it. He's breaking loose.

Fixed: by separating them out into two sentences, each ended with proper punctuation.

Your muscles are strong, your mind is weak.

comma splice: two complete sentences spliced together with a comma.

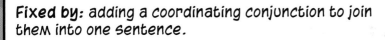

Your muscles are strong, but your mind is weak.

Fixed by: adding a coordinating conjunction to join them into one sentence.

THE DISAGREEMENT!

EVIL POWER:

THE DISAGREEMENT HAS THE POWER TO BLOCK THE TEAMWORK BETWEEN THE SUBJECT AND THE VERB OF A SENTENCE AND CAUSE THEM TO DISAGREE ON THEIR NUMBERS.

Every hero knows that sentences work better with teamwork, but this obnoxious character begs to differ. His name is the Disagreement, and as a super sour member of the Sabotage Squad, he much prefers conflict, contradiction, and confusion in your sentences. And that's why the Disagreement is constantly working to break up the teamwork between the subject and verb of a sentence.

Here's an example:

Our hero are powerful.

The sentence above is wrong. The Disagreement has blocked the teamwork between the subject and the verb so that their numbers (singular or plural) do not agree.

The subject of the sentence, "hero," is singular, but the verb, "are," is plural. The only way to fix this problem is by having the subject and the verb agree on their numbers.

For example, if our sentence has a singular subject, "hero," then it should have a singular verb, "is."

Our hero is powerful.

And, if our sentence has a plural subject, "heroes," then it should have a plural verb, "are."

Our heroes are powerful.

Now that the subject and verb of each sentence agree, each sentence, aside from making sense, is now correct.

An important part of the subject and verb's teamwork is agreeing on their numbers.

So, citizen, never forget that teamwork is the secret weapon, and this should be something that we can all agree on. Well, all of us except for the Disagreement.

SUPER EXAMPLES:

The robbers is stealing my money.

disagreement: plural subject: robbers (they), singular verb: is

The robbers are stealing my money.

agreement: plural subject: robbers (they), plural verb: are

We defends the world from evil.

disagreement: plural subject: We, singular verb: defends

We defend the world from evil.

agreement: plural subject: We, plural verb: defend

SUPER EXAMPLES:
WITH COMPOUND SUBJECTS:

The hero and his sidekick patrols the city.

disagreement: plural subjects: hero and sidekick (they), singular verb: patrols

The hero and his sidekick patrol the city.

agreement: plural subjects: hero and sidekick (they), plural verb: patrol

The Tiki Torch and Lava King makes a hot team.

disagreement: plural subjects: The Tiki Torch and Lava King (they), singular verb: makes

The Tiki Torch and Lava King make a hot team.

agreement: plural subjects: The Tiki Torch and Lava King (they), plural verb: make

Congratulations, citizen! You've completed the mission!

Now you're a part of the team. And with the Completion Team, the Amazing Eight, and the Super Symbols by your side, you'll always be able to defeat the treacherous Sabatoge Squad.

For more super missions, visit us at:

SUPERGRAMMAR.COM

Tony Preciado and Rhode Montijo are Illustrating the Point.

For my wife, Adrienne Anderson, and my daughter, Scarlett Danger
—Tony Preciado

For dedicated teachers, visual thinkers, and other superheroes
—Rhode Montijo

Super Thanks!

We'd like to thank all of the superheroes who came to our rescue and gave us the power we needed to make *Super Grammar*: Adrienne Anderson, Lynette Anderson, Christopher Hernandez, Rich Stim, Mary Flower, Jenny Hansen, Joe To, Jason Jaworski, Regina Preciado, Chris Goehe, and Abel Montijo.

We'd also like to thank Rick DeMonico, Paul Banks, Brenda Murray, and all the good people at Scholastic for their amazing teamwork and super support.